Timothy Otis Paine

Selections from the Poems of Timothy Otis Paine

Timothy Otis Paine

Selections from the Poems of Timothy Otis Paine

ISBN/EAN: 9783337407179

Printed in Europe, USA, Canada, Australia, Japan

Cover: Foto ©Andreas Hilbeck / pixelio.de

More available books at **www.hansebooks.com**

SELECTIONS

FROM

THE POEMS OF

TIMOTHY OTIS PAINE

G. P. PUTNAM'S SONS

NEW YORK   LONDON
27 West Twenty-third Street   24 Bedford Street, Strand

The Knickerbocker Press

1897

The Knickerbocker Press, New York

PREFACE.

THE poems in this small posthumous volume are a part of those written by the author in the intervals of a busy student life. I say student life, yet he was as intrinsically a poet as a student, and, to speak most truly, it seems as if his life were made of three, symmetrically united into one.

In the first place he was the active pastor, loving very much those he served for nearly forty years, and very much beloved by them.

Then he was the learned archæologist who restored Solomon's Temple, using as his implements the many languages he learned for the purpose ; employing, also, an artist power of illustration, so rare, so accurate, so exquisite, that the plates in his folio volume, beautiful as they are, are dwarfed by the original drawings from which they are taken. Thus, during a large portion of his working life, his thoughts dwelt in the world of the Scriptures, the Hebrew, the Septuagint, the Copt, the Italic, and that of the other authorities he consulted.

"I am all buried up in the visions of God in Ezekiel," he once wrote, "and in them I do know something—near—I know Ezekiel's heart."

As an archæologist he, also, followed, in the hieroglyphics of the *Book of the Dead*, what the Egyptians relate of the hereafter, and portrayed on a long scroll the journey of the spirit as there recorded.

His third life was that of the poet, and yet, as I have said, the poet was the underlying and ever-present man. He seemed always conscious of nature, and little in her realm escaped the keenness of his observation. He even caught the reflection of a violet in the clear eyes of a grazing cow. As a boy, he could call the birds to him, and he held converse with the trees and the streams.

The intense enthusiasm of his character was remarkable, an enthusiasm as far removed from temporary excitement as the steady glow of a planet is from the darting of a flame, and as great in his last, his seventy-second year, as it could have been in his youth. This seemed to preserve the unaffected heart of childhood in his gentle, useful age. It was, however, very individual, for it co-existed with calmness, and left the impression of knowing "the bit and the bridle." Akin to it, and giving it its aliment, was an equally remarkable appreciation of all greatness. A gigantic work of the human intellect, a new dictionary, for instance, an invention showing a new use of some law of nature, made him "catch fire at once," as he expressed it.

He loved to pay eloquent tribute to the real greatness of the simple, the unnoticed, the lowly. He admired especially work—fine and faithful—no matter how humble. This fine work he strove to give in all that he did. "Whosoever builds must do so in full faith;" he said, "for it seems to me not worthy of a man to work poorly, fearing that his work will perish. There is a great deal of work put into everything about us—even a snow-flake or the flower of a weed ; and the smallest object in nature is worked up as perfectly as the largest. It hurts the mind to work poorly ; and it helps the mind forever to do the least thing to the best."

No word was too homely for him, if it expressed his thought best, or named his fact. The scores of letters he wrote to be sure of accuracy in every detail of his *Woodlanders*, were as eager and interested as his researches for Solomon's Temple.

Of course, this rich, threefold life could not be attained without a withdrawal from much that occupies the world. In retired simplicity, with great concentration of purpose, he kept far from the interests of the mart and the exchange. His thought tarried little on the politics of the day.

No more could this life be attained had he not had a home in which he found perfect sympathy, rest, and renewal ; a home where he received as he gave, and where he still gives from beyond.

Thus he was enabled to sow by many waters. We know that a blessing has come from some of these poems ; may more blessings still spring from this seed that he has sown !

S. W. P.

CONTENTS.

CONTENTS.

CONTENTS.

FREE AND LOOSE.

I WILL sing where I light
   And alight where I may,
As the birds in their flight
   That go singing away.

Not a foot of the ground
   Do I own, not a hand ;
I go trespassing round
   For the flowers of the land ;

Not to pick anything,
   But to see them in bloom
And to hear the birds sing
   Where there 's plenty of room.

I

THE RAINBOW IN THE SPRAY.

ANOTHER present from Heaven,
   Another peaceful day ;
Like a dew that covers the dryness,
   Like a rainbow in a spray.
And this is all of my lifetime,
   And this my only day
That I need to think of or care for,
   With its rainbow in the spray.

SOUL-SONG.

I FEEL a song
Going by on the wind
Of the air that is breathed
    By the mind,

But hear no word
Of the lay as it flows
In a silvery stream
    To the close.

VIOLIN.

I AM a violin
    Missing the fingers slender
That whilom took me in
    To bosom tender;

Longing again to hear
    All of the dear caressings
And feel the gentle ear,
    The warm heart blessings.

Oh for the touch again
    Vibrating all the stringing
That silent must remain—
    To one hand ringing!

VIOLET BUTTERFLY.

LITTLE blue butterfly
   Like a blue violet,
Up from the meadow fly
   Like a blue violet.

What is it floateth thee,
   Lavender violet?
Where is it bearing thee,
   Soul of a violet?

5

SONGS OF THE INSECTS.

I HEAR the songs of the insects
Out in the dark to-night
Enter the open window
Of the chamber void of light;
And they come like words of comfort
Spoke to the darkened mind,—
Like the words so tenderly uttered
That opened the eyes of the blind :
And I feel me falling to slumber
In wondering over the way
The continuous tridulous singing
Is tingeing the dark with day.

SONG OF THE SNOW.

Far up in the depths of the sky,
In the loft of the zenith on high,
Under the top of the dome
Is the feathery snow's high home.

It is there that garments of white
Are suddenly made in the height
And dropped on the sorrowing throng
Who cry to the Lord, " How long ? "

And heads that are bowed and old
Grow white as the sheep of the fold—
As the crowns of the purified throng
Who reign with the Lord—how long !

AUTUMN TREES.

NATURE dresses her children best
Just before they fall to their rest ;
Puts on every beautiful vest
Ere they pass to the fields of the blest ;
Every fruit is fairest drest,
Every leaf is beautifulest.

TO THE BUTTERFLIES.

Ye are blessed, butterflies ;
Ye are of the early wise.
Now ye feed on tender leaf,
Now ye bide in durance brief,
And not over-long delay
To put forms meant for earth away.

SEEDS.

Round about upon the weeds
There are many little seeds
Held in many a tiny cup
Only waiting to come up :
Only waiting for the sun ;
For the winter to be done ;
For a bosom in the earth
Warm enough to give them birth.
And I feel like any weed
With a ripe or dropping seed ;
Waiting for another sun
When my little day is done.

THE LOST FLOWER.

FLOWERS that be so very small,
Flowers that be no flowers at all—
Not the size and not perfume
But the hand that held the bloom.

Fingers of the hand so small,
Fingers that are spirit all—
Not the hand, but 't is the thought
Moves the fingers unto aught.

Thought alone I value not
But the soul within the thought.—
Oh ye flowers out o'er the land,
How I miss the vanished hand !

MOSSES.

THE little mosses trusting cling
To all the ledges where they spring :
Content to live in lowly bed
Or honeysuckle rock o'erhead ;
Or in the vases of the ice,
Or where the trout brook taketh rise ;
Upon the wall, or on the tree,—
Where'er their happy home may be.

CHILDREN OF HEAVEN.

In Heaven we shall be children again ;
Children of One from children of twain.

None but children shall come into Heaven ;
Children of seventy, children of seven.

So it is said, and so it is sung :
As we grow older we shall grow young.

SONG OF MY LOVING.

I OFTEN think in the evening
  Or when the morning is near
Or in the twilight of sadness
  Why is it I am here ?
And why do I stay so long
  And steadily away ?
Why alway going to see them
  But never setting the day ?
My bosom is heaving and aching
  For the few that yet remain,
And I am longing and planning
  To see them once again. —
And also the day am I setting ?
  I have but few to set,
But send this song of my loving
  To those who have them yet.

THE BUILDER.

AH me, the step, how short a one,
Between the doing and the done !
How near the barque may come to land
Yet cast her cargo on the sand !

Oh give me strength, and give me mind
To finish what my hands may find !
That none may say, in future days,
This man could hew, but could not raise.

SWEET MEMORIES.

I THINK sweet memories will not die,
But live, and die not ever.
I think the hearts sweet memories tie
Will bounden be forever.
I think sweet memories will awake
That long have slept and slumbered.
I think the longest night will break
In dawn, and joys unnumbered.

THE OLD BRIDGE.

I SEE how long they will miss her :
   We are alway building new bridges ;
We raise up the old-time valley
   And level off the ridges.
The overarching elm trees
   Are killed by our new filling ;
But still we build new bridges
   And little heed the killing.
But do not believe, my darling,
   That so it will be with you :
My spirit goes over the old bridge
   And only my feet the new.

A WORM.

I CAME not down from Heaven
  Nor came I to my own ;
But I am born of earth
  To none in Heaven known.

Oh Who will give me might
  To break away and fly
That I be not a worm
  The day I die !

MANSIONS.

I AM glad that His house hath mansions,
　For I shall be tired at first ;
And I 'm glad He hath bread and water of life,
　For I shall be hungry and thirst.
I am glad that the house is His, not mine,
　For He will be in it, and near ;
To take from me the grief I have brought
　And to wipe away every tear.

WATERS OF THE MEADOW.

THE water on the meadow's breast
  Is moving slowly, as I look :
  She cannot yet be called a brook
   . But water seeking rest—
  Her level and her rest.

She is not seeking greater height,
  But willingly is moving slow
  And going where the ground is low :
    And yet her face is bright—
    Her face is calm and bright.

THE FOOT-TRACK.

THOUGH it with toil be rife
This is my way of life.

Though other roads are fair
They lead to otherwhere.

Though rugged be the path
It many restings hath.

When slacks the driver's rein
Then ends the old home lane.

ODE TO THE SUN.

GREAT gable-tipping sun,
  Just bursting from the east
Thy day is now begun.

But thou art not alone
  The builder of a day :
Each man shall make his own.

Oh, mightiest of the great,
  Alone in majesty,
Thou movest on in state !

But over thee and me
  There is a Mightier One
Who guideth me and thee.

The great alike and small,
  Attended or in wait,
Shall hearken to His call.

22

GOOD WORK.

WHO praised when sun, moon, star,
Great earth, and sea spread far
Were made ?   But yet what worth
From laboring sun, sea, earth !

Put work enough in all
Thou doest, great or small,
And let the ages tell
How much thou didst, and well.

, A SIGH.

My wounded heart is sore
　And needs a gentle touch :
　I do not ask for much
And cannot ask for more—
　A gentle touch.

BE CAREFUL.

Thou easily mayst crush the flower ;
The delicate thing is in thy power,
A ready victim of its doom :
But thou canst not restore its bloom.

THE BOAT.

To-morrow we will sail again *
    In our little boat.
'T will take but one to man the bark :
    'T is but a feeble float.
We shall row in waters then
Never seen afore ;
And we 'll drive our shallow skiff
To another shore.

* *Cras ingens iterabimus æquor.*—Horace.

I GREW OLD.

I GREW old, the other day,
And I worked uneasily.
Then I thought it need not be :
By and by we shall not say
" I grew old, the other day."

STONYTOP.

I KNOW the hills about old home
    But little higher are than these ;
And yet I cannot make it seem
    That this is so—with ease.

The scene from Stonytop is fair
    As that my childhood gazed upon ;
But youth comes falsifying things
    And this is all outshone.

These robins and the sparrows stir
    My heart as in the olden days ;
But much of glory in their songs
    Is from the early lays.

Deep in the oldest tree are veins
    That formed there when the trunk was young ;
But life comes gushing up through them
    The latest growths among.

ODE TO THE WIND.

Oh Wind of mighty will,
  Remember Him who spake
  To thee upon the lake
And once again be still !

Lift not the awful deep,
  Nor tumble it ashore,
  Nor scream above the roar,
Nor pile it heap on heap.

Without thy wilful rage
  The ocean were a glass :
  The birch canoe might pass
On it an endless age.

Oh had I not been cast
  Upon a wind-torn sea

How quiet might I be
And safe on land at last !

But so the Spirit goes
As blows the viewless wind,
Upheaving all the mind
And searching all her woes*;

Uptearing from its bed
And dashing on the beach
Along the sandy reach
The weedy crop and dead.

With mighty hand and high
And voice that terrifies
The obedient waves that rise
Confounded with the sky,

The Spirit in the breast
Sweeps on its rugged course,
An ocean-moving force,
And brings the bark to rest.

THE WHEAT OF AMENTI.

WILL men forget that my wheat-field
Was once full fresh and fair ?
Will they say that naught but stubble
And yellow straw are there ?
Will they forget the wheat-field
Was once full green and fair ?

I 've seen full many an image,
Carved on the Nile of old,
Of the travelling souls of Amenti
In their journeys manifold
Carrying wheat for which they had labored
While their life was yet on earth,
With the hoe of field and garden
And their name and symbol of worth :
And I 've wondered if Someone had told them
There is life in the earthly grain

That will make the meadows of Heaven
Look fresh and green again.

And I 've seen these souls of Amenti
With their hoe of garden and field
At work on the heavenly tillage ;
And I 've seen the heavenly yield
High rising above the reapers
Like reeds by the water side ;
And I 've seen their cattle threshing
In the Anro Meadow wide ;
And I 've seen their wheat unwinnowed
And their winnowed wheat, and bread,
With a spirit kneeling before One
Who hath a crown on His head !

And then I have thought of the question,
If the living point in the grain
Will put forth shoots in Amenti
Turning green my field again.

THE POOR WEED.

THERE are that fulfil not their promises.
The leaves are often fairer than the fruit ;
The tender infant fairer than the man.
But shall the infant lie within the man
As in a tomb of everlasting death ?
Or shall an Angel come and loose the door
And sit upon the stone ?   Oh child in me,
Cease not thine efforts once again to live
A second child, or child a second time :
Once child of earth, now child of heavenly clime.

WAIT.

Nature alway is in tune :
Nature alway hath a rune.
Let it be an autumn day ;
Let it be a day in May :
Nature alway hath a rune ;
Nature alway is in tune.
Let it be in autumn late :
There is music when we wait.
Once I waited very long ;
But my life became a song.

END OF DECEMBER.

Spring is a lisper ;
Comes in a whisper.
Spring is a tumming,
Tapping and thrumming.
Coming a little,
Moiety, a tittle ;
For the December
Is but an ember.

WINTER CHICKADEES.

Now the winter chickadee
Flutters in the appletree,
On the bole and on the bough,
On the frosty foggage now,
While the sun is held with ease
Right between two sinewy trees.

Now he singeth " chickadee ; "
" Phebe," now, and plaintively ;
Now another sweeter lay
Few would think his song or say :
Song or say of nesting time
When sweet love is in her prime.

BREAKING UP OF WINTER.

LITTLE squirrel, spring is hatching ;
Love and happiness are catching.
Now the river-ice is broken ;
The Ticonic Falls have spoken ;
Segur and the Clover woken.
Fort Hill now is showing patches
Large enough for partridge scratches.
Ducks are in the breathing places
Where the fishes sun their faces.
Peetweets soon will be repeating
All their rapid, high peetweeting ;
River-bank to bank o'erflitting,
On the river-boulders sitting,
Teetering up and down and quitting.
Many things will soon be coming ;
Bees and bumblebees a-humming.
There 's enough to keep us happy
In our burrows warm and nappy.

TO THE BLUEBIRD.

Oh dearest birds that ever sang,
　That ever sang and made a nest,
Ye bluebirds, flying round in pairs,
　I love you, faithful bluebirds, best.

From early spring to autumn snow
　In hollow post or rail ye build ;
Or, on the corner of the barn
　Your little box with straw is filled.

Oft, going for the pastured cow,
　I 've turned me to the old stump fence
To see your blue eggs in a root
　Or if the young had fluttered thence.

38

Ye turtle doves of northern homes,
   Of northern homes on either hand,
Your simple note, so soft and deep,
   Will soon be heard out o'er the land.

ROBIN-SONG.

THE robin sings at dimmy dawn,
At any time all day,
And when the twilight cometh on
You hear the robin-lay.
All while the robin is awake,
With time for leisure wing,
He 'll sit and sing for singing's sake,
Nor sigh if he can sing.
And when a grief is overpast
He 'll seek the topmost bough
And sing as he would sing his last,
As he is singing now.
To-day he loves the sunny sun,
To-morrow loves the rain,
In autumn loves the winter run,
And loves the spring again.

He thinketh not if he may die,
Or mourneth the unknown,
But feels the moment going by
And maketh it his own.

CHIMNEY SWALLOW.

HITHER comes the swallow back,
   Doing as I knew he would :
Wing and body picked, black,
   Chitting round in cheery mood ;
Lighting ne'er on roof or tree,
   Twittering ever on the wing :
Note, but ne'er a song hath he ;
   Chats, like me, but cannot sing.
And he knoweth naught of earth,
   Feeding in the wingy air ;
Lighting just above the hearth,
   For his little home is there :
Skimming in a morn of May
   In a mellow, mackerel sky ;
Up, and off, and high away,
   Disappearing to the eye :

Then our little bird will come—
Robin never lived so near—
Down into the heart of home,
Filling it with quiet cheer.

TO THE WOOD–THRUSH OF SEGAGUS.

Shy thrush, again thy voice is heard,
Thou sweetest, lonest, native bird,
Emperchèd out of reach of gun,
But plainer seen, marked by the sun,
The setting sun, here out of sight,
But not to thee in that far height,
As still thou singest, singest long,
Upon thy crimson mount of song,
A little island high away
Retaining all there is of day,
And all the choicest thing on earth,
A wood-thrush, heir of song by birth.
    Where didst thou pass thine infancy?
What food ambrosial nourished thee?
Wert cradled in the purple clouds,
Or in the wreath of mist thee shrouds,

44

Or housened on the braken sward,
Thou spirit, looking heavenward ?
    Thou 'mindst me of my mate, my bird,
Whose richest tones at eve are heard ;
As once, adown this woodland green,
Thine own self, vying, well hast seen.
Thou markedst how she moved along
In the full current of thy song,
As thou wert watching, overhead,
Thine each note pulsing in her tread,
Alternate listening to her tone,
And, next time, deepening thine own.
    And now the eve is coming on
And thy last sunbeams almost gone
Upon the dark top of the pine,
Thy little form alone in shine ;
A little crescent, setting moon,
A while in sight, but lost too soon ;
A wood-thrush warbling deeper still
As evening shades Segagus' rill
And one sense less distracts the mind

From sweet sounds floating on the wind :
A meteor starting into sight
And gliding down into the night
Thou comest, darling, from the tree
To sit and carol nearer me.

THE EAGLE.

How the eagle does :—
   Gathering up his might,
Quitting where he was,
   Soars he in the height.
But his aerie home
   Is not alway grand :
Now on mountain dome,
   Now in lowly land.
In a rugged wold,
   Be it but apart,
He shall build his hold,
   Take his mighty start.
Where he makes his bed,
   Where he piles his lair,
Turns his noble head,
   'T is the king that 's there.

Where he heaps his nest,
　Where he lies in state,
Where he takes his rest,
　There the place is great.
When he looketh far
　Through the forest dim
From a naked spar,
　Then look up at him.
Feel him seize thine eye ;
　See him once for aye ;
Watch him towering high
　On his spiral way,
Till, a little mote,
　Black upon the blue,
He is like a boat
　Sailing out of view.

WREN.

LITTLE chubby, twittering wren,
In the eastern home again
Soon wilt build the hasty bed
Round the gray old barn or shed,—
In a mortise of a brace,
Bluebird box, or other place
Large enough for bumblebee,
Or, my feather-ball, for thee.

Wonder if you, little pest,
Still fill up the bluebird's nest
Now with straw, and now with twig,
Till the hole is not so big
As the bluebird's darling head ;
Stealing from her her sweet bed,

49

Forcing her to work for you
A whole precious day or two ?—
So insultingly a chip
On the gable's very tip
While the bluebird is gone in ;
Stopping quick your ceaseless din
When the bluebird flies away,
Hurrying in whate'er you may.
Are there, darling as thou art,
Some to take the bluebird's part,
Pulling out your barnyard stuff
Till the hole is large enough
For the bluebird, rightful host,
On the barn's high corner-post ?
Oh how often I 've regretted
That thy ways me ever fretted !
We have been so rudely parted
Oh how oft I grow sad-hearted !
Could we meet and never part
I would love thee as thou art,—
Filling every nook with crannies,

Helping you, whate'er your plan is,
Favoring all your fancies pretty
Never wearying of your ditty ;
Making boxes without number
Out of gray old fencing lumber,
Nailing them where'er their tint
Gives the seeker little hint :
Or upon the oilnut gray,
Cool, and from the cat away,
Or about the eaves and gable
Of the house or shed or stable.

Oh could we live o'er again
All our childhoods, little wren,
There 'd be room enough for more
Than there was in days of yore !

ODE AND SONG TO THE ENGLISH SPARROW.

HAIL to thee, Terror,
Brought by an error,
Fancy, or notion,
Over the ocean,
     Sparrow of England !

How is it Ayrshire,
Dumfries, and Her'shire
Have yet a wood-bird,
Bad bird or good bird
If the whole country is
Full of thy effronteries,
     Pet pest of England ?

———

So round about our hedges flit ;
Deep in the cedars crowd and chit.

When Winter frays each other wing,
Here do thy very best to sing :
Make happy noise in merry time,
A flood of noise instead of rhyme,
And break the Winter all to bits,
Ye little busy foreign chits.

THE BAT.

Thou, little even bird,
Seen dimly and unheard ;
Too poor to fire at,
Thou nothing but a bat !
I get a mighty word :—
Be little seen and heard.
  Oft as at eventide
I walk the riverside
I view thee catching flies
All round about the skies :
All using up the day
And not in any's way.
  When sparrows under hill
Are chippered out and still
And Silence, like a mist,
Signs to the meadow " Hist ! "

'T is perfectness in thee
To move so silently.
    And when the sky is red
And thou art overhead,
And when it 's toning down
And shading into brown,
'T is well thou autumn bit
Art blended into it.

THE MYSTIC.

THE violet blows by Mystic side
   When all the leaves are tender,
And on her fells, a day in June,
   The honeysuckle slender.

The violet blooms in Segur Dell,
   And there I wander early
To guess if honeysuckles blow
   By one I love so dearly.

The common ocean gathers in
   The Mystic and the Segur,
And where the stormy petrel flits
   Unites their waters eager.

They rise in mist, they fall in rain,
   In dew, and sunny showers,

And glide as one in Segur Dell
   Beneath the spreading bowers.

But little hope is there for me
   That I may meet the maiden
Who looked at me and spoke to me
   Then left me lone and laden.

SHAWS OF THE SEGUR.

THE Segur Shaws are beckoning me ;
Their sacred walks are o'er the lea ;
And Sabbath hangs her holy veil
    Around the shaws for me :

For love of one hath holy feet
And love of her to-day is meet :
Two silent souls in quietude,
    O grant communion sweet !

Let love and joy the far-off maid,
In secret chamber closed, invade,
And move her thought in wondering way
    To Segur's slaty glade.

The peace of all this fragrant dell
Enfold her spirit in a spell,

Albeit the place unknown, undear
    As he who loveth well.

But once we met, and parted then—
So long ago I know not when :
We parted then and met no more
    And little heard again.

Yet still I come to Segur braes
With oaken shaws and braken sprays,
To still brood o'er one memory
    So sacred all the days.

VISIT TO SEGUR'S BROOK.

I once, O Segur, hoped to sing
A song for all the ages ;
But now I cannot, e'en in prose,
Tell what my heart encages.
The trees grow nobler all along
Thy crooked, winding valley,
And June is sweeter than a song
As breezes die and rally.
There 's listening on every hand
For something to be uttered :—

" O Segur, speak the lover's love
So often to thee muttered :
The love of one as far away
As in his early childhood
Still filling all his heart with love

And all this listening wildwood.
Oh cease thy carol, sacred thrush,
Thou bird of all the ages !
I cannot bear the mighty strain
That now my heart engages.
Oh speak aloud ye human trees
A hundred feet above me ;
Your dewy eyes and trembling lips
Reveal how well ye loved me !
Ye Seba Heights and Segur Hills,
Three Heights and Hills scarce parted,
Low in the centre at your feet
Bear witness ' One true hearted.' "

A DEW-DROP.

One sun-lit dew-drop in the grass ;
No other anywhere in sight :
Some gentle fairy, in her pass,
Out of her necklace droppèd it last night.

And now it is a sapphire blue ;
And now a yellow topaz fair ;
And now a ruby drop of dew :
What kind of jewel doth a fairy wear?

THE EVENING PRIMROSE.

THE primrose blooms at eventide,
And, where I go, the highway side'
It lights up with its yellow blow :
What else it does I do not know,—
Except, all day, with dust of road
The leaves are gray, and, until blowed,
The bud is gray, with slight perfume,
Till eve unfolds a clean sweet bloom.

It grows there in the short green grass
Between where foot and carriage pass :
Where wheels might crush it, should one ride,
And the horse startled sheer aside.
It sprang up there, and there hath grown
And made the narrow green its own :
Chose not a place by nature fair,

But made one so by growing there.
And when the August days are hot
It quitteth not the chosen spot,
But there at evening may be found
Because the root is deep in ground.

I often pick one for my wife ;
' T is so much like her own dear life
To stay right here where she but must
And be a flower though there be dust.

THE IMMORTAL TREE.

A TREE, delighted with the earth, grew sad
Because she must quite perish at the last.
Just then her seeds like myriad windows oped
Therewith, her eyes, and through them lookèd she
And saw herself an endless forest stand.
Then were content, but that another glance
Showed all her kind no longer on the earth,
Save deep in mines.   Her second sight was oped,
And she in her own proper person stood
A spirit tree within a spirit wood.
Then gladder grew her life ; and lop of bough,
Or loss of leaf or fruit she little marked ;
For that she felt herself all whole within,
However worn or spoilèd she had been.

MILE-STONES.

TRUE fame is worthy of a good man's zeal :
Confess it, ye who quicken at the names
Whose deeds or writ divide the distant past
Like mile-stones scattered on the closing way ;
Admonitory that the onward road
Will claim like bounds for yet back-looking man.
How much we owe unto the garnered past !
Our lips to-day are not more surely fed
With last year grain than are our thinking souls
By old experience : by deeds and words
That were so done and writ, their echoes roll
Back from the luminous sky of olden days
With inward power to move us on our ways.

FORGETFULNESS.

I SEE not now why e'en forgetfulness
Should 'minish aught the joy the blessed feel,
Rich in the present filled to perfectness.
How few the memories we would bear to Heaven !
It being so, how much would we recall ?
How much regret spend over memories closed ?
These summer leaves may rattle to the earth,
But fruits matured are gathered to the barn.
And fruits have in them seeds to germinate
In other ground and yield like fruits again.
Nor shall aught die. The book of life here writ
Upon our inner selves stands legible
From age to age, a record foul or fair ;
And he that writeth needs but look in there.

HOME LAKE.

I 'M like a fish of the ocean,
   This rustling autumn day,
Remembering with emotion
   The lake of infancy,
Where now the painter, October,
   Oft looks and turns to me,
With face upraised and sober
   From her palate in the tree ;
And up the river of childhood
   My thoughtful way I take,
And up the streams of the wildwood
   And back into the lake.

TÉWELÉMA.

Princess Mássasóit,
Daughter of the chieftain,
Long descended, hail I
Thee the lineal ruler
Of these natal wildwoods.

The Satucket River
And her bordering valleys
And the hills above them
Crowned by Wónnocoóto
Claim their pristine monarch.

Spindles of the cornfield
Fingers multitudinous
To the Indian heavens,

Silent and unanimous,
Raise in attestation.

Every year the flowers,
With traditional memory
Of thy great grandsire
And new childlike wonder,
Open to behold thee.

And the great-eyed squirrel
In the sinewy oak top,
Mindful of thy fathers,
Holds the acorn breathless
Watchful of thy fingers.

I, too, lore instructed,
See the awful moccason
On thy foot imperial,
And dread Métacómet
Rises up in vengeance.

In the flying car train,
Sitting at a window

Looking on the woodland,
Thoughts of Oúsaméquin
Smooth thy troubled forehead.

Merciful and pitying
Was the mighty peace king
Sent to make it easy
For the band of pilgrims
Driven to thy forests.

In thy crown of feathers,
Lonely Téweléma,
Thou art going silent
To the Náhteawámett
On the Aśsowámsett ;

To the Reservation
Held by old tradition ;
Woótonékanúskè
And thy aged mother
Looking from the cabin.

Gone to the Ponémah
We shall miss you absent.
When the sparrow twitters
Then will we remember
Thee, O Chić-chic-chéwee.

And when fairs are crowded
On the Nunckatésett,
Then thou, Indian maiden,
Shalt appear in vision
From the isles of chieftains.

THE WOODLANDERS.

A LAMENT OVER THEM.

Ho, come, stand with heads uncovered
And hear the story told growing old !
   How men went to war as to pleasure
   As they go to seaside and mountain !
   How died they like flowers of the summer
That appear for a day and are gone !

I saw, out of Maine's pine forest,
The wood-camp crew on dead heavy tread :
   Not marching from schoolhouse to common,
   From common to schoolhouse returning,
   But forward and onward and southward
To the banks of Potomac away.

Old mates, crossing o'er at Fairfield
The Kennebec's proud wave, to the grave
  High travelling, musket to shoulder ;
  I saw them in columns unsorted,
  In ranks like the tips of the pine tops,
Short and tall, arm to arm, friend to friend.

Oh men, share my aching sorrow.
Bow down with grief profound to the ground.
  They never marched back again homeward ;
  They died on Virginia's borders ;
  The boughs of their bunks from the hemlock
Shed their leaves and dried up and decayed.

Ho, hear : 't is a piteous story :—
The forestmen are dead, they are sped.
  Their cabin of logs in the woodland
  Was glad with their yarns and their laughter ;
  They all slept together like children
With their feet to the open wood fire.

But now, rattling at his stanchion,
The ox looks round to hark in the dark :
 He hears not a sound that 's familiar ;
 He knows not the man in the hay-house ;
 Turns backward and forward his ears
And his eyes meet the eyes of his mate.

There 's grief when the cattle wonder
And moo and look about in a doubt :
 They die without reading their riddle ;
 They miss the old teamsters in exile ;
 See not the old cook with the lanterns
But the new one bring lights for the teams.

Ah say, Where is now the story
That whiled the evening long like a song ?
 The teller was off for the war-camp ;
 The hearer sprang up from the telling
 At once with the shriek of Fort Sumter
When the cannon was fired at her flag.

Oh woe when the story 's broken
Beside the burning heap ere men sleep :
For who could go on with the wonder
When seats by the fireside are vacant
And hearers would only be thinking
Of the voice of the mate who began ?

And weep o'er the single hearted
Who alway live at home, summer home,
And sleep in the woods in the winter,
And then from the quiet of nature
Are marched through bewildering cities
To the lonely wild waste of the war.

————

Gone, gone, and a border soldier.
How far away from home thou dost roam.
How cruel the soul to the body
To bear it a captive so hopeless.
Dost never thou feel for a moment
Any sickness for home in the woods ?

Come back.   Now the snow is fallen ;
'T is eighty feet on high in the sky ;
   The pine tops are loaded down heavy ;
   'T is level arm deep on the leaf bed ;
   The cook has piled high the tea fire
And is waiting and watching for you.

The meal soon will be all ready ;
In half a minute more or before :
   Rake open the fire and the ashes ;
   Dig down for the beans in the embers ;
   The biscuit are brown in the bakers
And the dippers are brought for the tea.

Oh say, Will ye come to supper ?
Does home look good afar where ye are ?
   Come ! Axes are swinging and ringing
   And echoing clear to the table,
   'Mid calls of the men and the crashings
And the singing of saws and the chains.

I see, in among the pine trees,
The flannel sleeves and red, hear the tread
  Of men with their axes to shoulder,
  Each man with an axe on his shoulder,
  At will bearing arms of the log-land
To the peaceful and quiet home hut.—

Alas, they be ghosts and phantoms,
The shadows of the great in a strait
  That vanished one day from the forest.
  I saw, in the long heavy car-train,
  Their regiment stop for a little,
And I asked who they were and where bound :

" O guard, let me look a moment."
I saw the men in blue two and two ;
  In every car-seat twin messmates,
  And never a car-seat was empty,
  Bent forward and resting their foreheads ;
And they looked like a thousand of lions.

No more.   Went they on and onward.
I heard the cannon sound ; and the ground
   Was alway in opening her bosom
   And folding them mustered from battle.
   But off were their wraiths to the wildwood,
Their freed manes were back in old home.

Even now, when the snow is going,
And logs are hauled no more to the shore,
   And axes no longer all talking,
   Their shades wander down over State Street
   And into the city of Bangor
With the sturdy old stepping of yore.

Like beeves, free of yoke and loosened,
Together keep they still down the hill,
   Along by the Bridge of Kenduskeag,
   To Elder's, the Alleyway Cellar,
   And eat of the meal they had promised
Far away in the fields of the South.

THE LOST SHEEP.

Hear, Good Shepherd, hear my cry ;
Lost among the hills am I.
Leave, for me, the ninety-nine ;
Find me, find, and make me thine.
In the mountains, strayed from thee,
Come, O come, and seek for me.

Where the wilderness is dry
Seek for me before I die.
Where the mountain-side is steep
And ravines are dark and deep,
Where thou hearest one low moan
Seek me starving, lost, and lone.

Lay me on thy shoulders, lay,
Weak and weary of my way.

All my strength in wandering spent,
Take, and bear me to thy tent.
Let me hear thine own dear voice,
And thy friends, with thee, rejoice.

MEASURE.

A LONG, low line of brick and granite stores
Extended down a river's narrow vale.
These blocks were built full fifty years ago ;
But failure following swiftly on their rise
They died in youth, a row of skeletons
Wherein the ghosts of disappointed men
Held nightly haunt among decaying stairs
And lookèd out through empty window holes.
The region was a place one went to see
And then to think of in the dead of night.
It was a weird retreat that wound away
As wound the stream which dully rippled by.
So little trodden was it that the weeds
Came up among decaying lumber-piles.
The dandelion blossomed here in May

In crevices of long neglected walks.
The street was like a discontinued road
Where daisies, buttercups, and grasses grow.
Boats paddled by, and all was still again.
The meditative boy who came to fish
Forgot to bait his hook and went to sleep
Among the flowers with gentle Solitude.
The city noises, busy in their place,
Ne'er thought to turn aside and come in here,
But here it was a workman wandered in,
Like some lone bird, and built his hidden nest.
Old Time alone took rent in every room ;
Thought quartered here ; Invention here abode ;
Patience had chambers ; Trying stayed here long ;
Measure, the snow-white queen of perfect work,
Her golden reed borne in her lily hand,
Here sought her child, and said, " Take this, my son,
And fix its perfect marks the first since time.
Guide every hand henceforth through ways untried
And haste the coming of the coming age."
She reached to him her reed and disappeared,

But did not leave his side until Success,
With clean and radiant robes, stripped off the clothes
Work-worn and mean, but beautiful to those
Who knew the workman and the work he wrought.

'T is measure leads straight on to perfect fit ;
And perfect fit is perfect perfectness.
Who marks the perfect rule helps read the stars.
The slightest fault on earth is great in heaven :
The line that deviates will never reach
The targe where Truth, the Revelator, stands.
The perfect Rule is Empress of the hand :
" Work thus," she saith, " from needle-point to
        point ; "
And men of master mind obey her word.
Mechanic and astronomer are one ;
Astronomer and captain of the ship ;
Captain and mate ; the mate and pilot, one ;
Pilot and sailor ; men, and instruments
That look up to the skies, or tell the time,
Or feel the cold and heat and weigh the air
That lie between the sundered continents.

'T is accuracy of guidance and of aim
That swings the planets of the universe
In wavy lines without one accident.
'T is guidance through a point that hath no length
Which microscope can see, and then the point
That lieth next thereto, and then the next,
That bears a hundred million suns upon
Their unknown course with rifle-bullet speed
Attended by their planetary earths
Like flocks of birds that cross the summer sky,
Without one wrecking crash, or hit, or jar :
Without one sound so loud as of a bee
That shoots herself away unto the hive.
'T is perfectness of work makes silence reign
Among the myriad stars. 'T is perfect work
To turn a shaft on nothing ; to revolve
Each glittering globe of fire with solid core
Around a line more slight than spider-web ;
On pivots smaller than the sting of bee ;
On axle-bearings that no bearings are—
Mere points of turning that shall know no wear
As untold ages wend through endless time.

The Builder of the boundless universe
Creates in man an image of Himself ;
And keeps created there and keeps alive
The power to build the countless miniatures
Of perfect work ; until a thousand wheels
Grow silent, or, grow still, and stiller grow,
In imitation of the moving worlds.

'T is perfect measure forms the telescope
That finds the angle for a new result ;
And this result guides every struggling ship
To port and home : the sailor's life is hung
On accurate measurement.   'T is point by point
Our lives are measured off.   The ticking watch
Proclaims our passing days : each tick, a day.
The escapement of a clock goes meting out
Our time.   With fingers on our wrist we feel
Escapement-work and know it is our own :
But joyful know the measuring is divine
And will not cease, but still go beating on,
Moved by His heart who moveth all that moves.

Our souls, like planets, know not where to go,
But follow on in floating, curving lines,
Now up, now down, to left, to right, but on ;
Our safety certain only as we yield.
But as we yield, the Great Astronomer
Of souls, with joyous calculation, sees
The peaceful path through which he can us lead.
Our path is holy ground.   By step and step
Is meted all our way.   Our road is by
A slowly winding stream ; and at our side
A man with flaxen line and measuring reed
Goes forth to measure down the narrow vale
And show the depth our life thus far hath gained :
Pauses at times and onward metes again
Until the stream becomes a river, and
A flood that none can cross.   So let it be :
The depth is alway equal to our day.
It hath been ever.   We are told not all :
A little now revealed ; and now a mite,
A morsel, hath been given unto us ;
A cup of water, then a crossless stream ;

And fruits are on the banks for every month.
But if so be the builders me reject
As stone unfitted, though bewrought with toil,
Are pillars only needed ?   Are not stones
For base and cornice, frieze and architrave,
For pavement, gates, and walls about the courts
And deep foundations needed each in place ?
May we nor seek the highest nor the low,
Nor seek at all save only to go in ?
For e'en the sparrow and the swallow find
Where they may nest and watch the worshippers.

The fane is measured, and the worshippers ;
The court, left out, unmeasured, given up
Unto the nations—all must fit the fane.
All forms are measurable ; and the lost
Are known, revealed, and fixed again to sight
By lines exact, exactly in their place.
But who shall find the measures I have lost—
The measures of a man ?   The length and breadth
And height must equal be.   Length is a line,

A hair, a viewless thread. The largest plane
Is but a surface that no thickness hath :
The length and breadth and height alone, a cube.
We must all measures have, and equal ones.
The sculptor measures in the marble block
And finds a man. The architect will seek,
With rule exact, and find a living shaft.
But oh what sculptor, architect, shall search
With line and reed, and beat away the chips,
And find a worshipper, or living stone,
To fit in somewhere in the holy fane !

www.ingramcontent.com/pod-product-compliance
Lightning Source LLC
Chambersburg PA
CBHW032156010726
47493CB00008BA/2720